Seriously???

COLLECTION OF SHORT STORIES

by Dannetta Sherray Holmes-Hollins

DORRANCE PUBLISHING CO
EST. 1920
PITTSBURGH, PENNSYLVANIA 15238

Dorrance Publishing Co
585 Alpha Drive
Suite 103
Pittsburgh, PA 15238
Visit our website at www.dorrancebookstore.com

ISBN: 979-8-88812-236-5
eISBN: 979-8-88812-736-0

Table of Contents

ACKNOWLEDGMENTS

THIS IS TO SHOW MY DEEPEST GRATITUDE TO SEVERAL PEOPLE WHOSE WORDS OR ACTIONS INSPIRED ME TO BE THE "BEST ME" IN 2023 AND BEYOND. EVEN IF WE CROSSED PATHS AS FAMILY, FRIENDS, OR IN THE VIRTUAL WORLD; IF YOU HAD ANY POSITIVE SIGNIFICANCE IN MY LIFE, I WANT EVERYONE TO SEE AND KNOW. THANK YOU SO MUCH.

SERIOUSLY???

"I sent this girl to school to get a college education and she comes steppin' up in here with a nI%@# old as me."

RIP Daddy, George H. Jr.

"If you really want something, you will work HARD to get it. You won't let anything stand in your way."

My Mother, Vivian H.

"I'm going all the way to the top and I'm takin' you with me. Gonna give it to you like God gave it to Moses, a little bit at a time."

My Husband, Tracy H.

"Two of my biggest supporters and inspiration. I love you."
Kendrick and Tracie H.

"You're one of the vehicles that Jehovah will use to make our family wealthy. I am so proud to call you my little sister."
My Brother, George H. III

"Nobody comes into our lives with STUPID stamped across their foreheads! We don't find that out till later."
My Sister, Angela H.

"To my brothers and sisters, thank you for your love and support always."
Sharon B, Katherine W., Willie H., and RIP Andre H.

"Don't live by other people's consequences; don't ask a question if you're not prepared to hear the answer."
My Closest and Dearest Friend, Ornetta W.

"What is your life's Blueprint?"
The Reverend Dr. Martin Luther King Jr.

"How can you cry about someone when they die, and give them HELL everyday while they're here? Respect me while I'm here."
Kwame H. Brown

"Seriously???, when are you going to start your channel? I think you will do very well."
It's Just Gems—-formerly Gems from Kwame Brown

*"To have a **conscience** is to know. I can accept you in truth, I can love you in truth. The discord comes when you force me to go against my own conscience."*
Angela Stanton King

"I want it to STING !!!—I want to drive you to achieve. Achieve something; large or small, make it something."
Queen Regina

"To all of my true friends in Missouri, I thank you so much."
**Shawnta R., Tonya L., Jessica J., Laura A.,
Angela Townsend-J., and Teresa S.**

"The Blue Cross Blue Shield Organization 2006-2011."
You Know Who You Are

"Stay in your lane. Don't come in my lane with nonsense."
Karceno4Life

"Seriously???, you better be out there handling your business."
Sister T.

"Don't be distracted. Stay on your path. They gonna hate on everything you do."
The Mil Ticket

"It's nothin' to it Seriously??? Just do it."
Toccara Tomorrow

"Keep going. Nothing but a beautiful future awaits us. Remain faithful. Stay encouraged."
Very Close Friend, Vickie E.

"To my childhood and high school friends. Thank you always for your support."
Laura B. and Michelle W.

"Don't count the days. Make the days count."
Forgotten Kingz TV. 2.0

"Friendship gives wings to the heart; as there is no difference that can set them apart."
Very Close Friend, Anita P.

"Your value is worth red corals and beyond."
Very Good Friend, C.L. Wade

REUNITED

Glenda searched endlessly for her new red pumps she had just purchased two weeks prior. *This would have to happen on this day of ALL DAYS*, she thought. *I specifically bought those shoes for this dress, now I'll be forced to change."* As she proceeded to her bedroom to find another outfit, she noticed her cell phone flashing on the kitchen counter. "Whomever that is, they'll just have to wait," she mumbled to herself. "I'm already pressed for time."

Giving herself a once-over before she left, Glenda smiled in admiration. "Not bad for a forty-something, almost divorced workaholic who hasn't been out in ages. I just might get asked to dance." As she grabbed her keys and phone from the counter, she was halted in her tracks by a text and a few missed calls. The text read:

Please call me back at this number, Glenda. It's very important. I know that I am the last person you would ever want to hear from at this time, but it's important that I speak with you. You are still my wife at least for now, that is.

Preston

Glenda was at a loss for words. She placed the phone back onto the counter to contain herself. For months, she and her estranged husband, Preston, have been embattled in a bitter divorce. Her heart was racing as she gained her composure. "I will not respond," she whispered. "Whatever he has to say to me can be directed to my attorney."

"So you're not going to see what he wants Glen?" asked Reeva. "It might be something beneficial. You might even get him to agree with what you want."

Glenda took another swig out of her Long Island. "I am not playing games with Preston any longer, Reeva. This mess should've been over. I don't have anything to say to him; that's what I pay Jarrett for."

The two ladies continued to sip their drinks and nod their heads to the music.

"Glenda, that's my song. I'm not missin' this jam. Reeva guzzled the rest of her drink and hurried to the dance floor. It wasn't long before she was accompanied by a handsome suitor; and they danced together as if they had known each other for years.

Look at Reeva, Glenda thought, smiling, *actin' like she's twenty-five. I'm not mad at her, though. We both deserve this night out.*

At that moment, Glenda felt her phone vibrating in her purse.

"This had better be important," she mumbled, "calling me at this hour."

The music was blaring nonstop, making it impossible for Glenda to hear inside of the club. She asked the doorman to stamp her wrist for re-entry as she made her way outside to take the phone call.

Glancing at the number, she noticed it was the same one from earlier, where Preston had texted from.

"Glenda Nell, please don't hang up. Just here me out. I know we're getting divorced, but I don't want us to end this way. Together for twenty-two years, that ought to count for something." The silence was deafening. "Hello?" replied Preston. "Are you still there, Glenda?"

Glenda cleared her throat. "Preston, this is water under the bridge. Let it go. You made your choice. It's obvious Anita meant more to you than I ever did. The only thing I expect from you now is to continue paying for Laythan's tuition at Wharton and our agreed-upon thirty percent of the shares in the company; everything else 'equally split.'"

Preston interjected. "What if I said I wanted my wife back? There is no amount of money or shares that can replace love. I never stopped loving you, Glenda. I'm willing to do whatever it takes to get us back together. I can sell the company; we can move to Philly to be closer to our son as he finishes school. You know Anita didn't mean anything to me; it was just a three-year fling that went terribly wrong. We can go to counseling. You can take that early retirement, Glenda; you always talked about retiring before sixty. I know we can make it work, baby; please give us another chance."

Glenda sat holding the phone in silence. After a two-year long "war of the roses" he was actually asking for a reconciliation.

"I can't talk to you right now, Preston." She hung up the phone abruptly, said a small prayer and reentered the nightclub.

Driving home, Glenda was so overwhelmed about the proclamation from Preston that she fought hard to hold back the tears. "How dare that bastard have the audacity to want to work things out after all the mayhem he's caused. I could never trust him. He could just one day decide again that our marriage is not enough and go into a 'midlife crash and burn' for a second time. And the devastation he caused our son for—Pete's Sake! Not willing to risk gettin' bit by the same dog twice."

Glenda pulled into her garage. *My mind is made up,* she thought. *There's no way I could live with myself if I take Preston back; far too much damage. Things are better off like they are. I'll give him my answer tomorrow.*

Glenda's Saturday morning jog seemed a bit longer than normal. Her mind was racing, and she was extremely rest-broken from the night before. Preston had called her more than five times already, leaving messages and texts, begging for her to forgive him, and wanting his family back.

Glenda finally put her silence to rest.

Let's meet at Paxton's for lunch, she replied via text. *We can discuss everything face-to-face. See you around one o'clock.*

Preston responded without haste. *See you there.*

When Glenda arrived, she was immediately escorted to the bar area by the hostess. "He's been waiting for you," the hostess explained. "He described your car, so I knew who to look for when you arrived."

Glenda feigned a smile as she took a seat across from Preston in the booth.

"Wow," he said. "You sure look a lot better than the last time we saw each other in mediation; you're not frowning. You look gorgeous." He presented her with a bouquet of "Ingrid Bergman" roses. "I still remembered these are your favorite."

"Get to it, Preston." She scowled. "I don't have all day. You were quite the talker when you were blowing my phone up all night."

Preston smiled and shook his head. "Baby, I made it perfectly clear what I wanted; I want you, the marriage, and our lives back. I have learned my lesson, Glenda. I am forty-nine years old; there comes a time in a man's life when he has to let go of childish things. I know I hurt you, but I am going to make everything right. Whatever you want for us, whatever you decide; I want to spend what's left of my life making it up to you…."

With those words, Preston grabbed Glenda's left hand. He reached into his shirt pocket and presented her with a three carat princess cut diamond ring. Glenda was at a loss for words, but the tears in her eyes made up for what her mouth couldn't say.

"Forgive me, Glenda, I am asking for you to forgive me. Whatever I need to do, wherever I need to go. I just want my wife back. We need to be a family again, baby. I never stopped loving you; you are my love. There is no other woman for me. If I have to die trying—"

In an instant, three gunshots rang out. Restaurant patrons and workers were screaming, taking cover, or running for the door. Once the calamity was tapering off, there stood a young woman; brandishing a gold-plated Smith and Wesson.

"I'm sitting here carrying your baby, while you're professing your undying love for your wife. I put up with that mess from you and Anita after you told me it was the last time. Here I'm thinking you're about to propose to me and you're trying to get back with your wife; as I waited almost three years for you to get divorced. I let you make a fool of me, Preston."

The mystery lady stood callously over the bodies of Preston and Glenda; she grabbed a cloth napkin and wiped blood from Glenda's hand.

"And give me this ring!" she screamed. "You won't be needing it where you're going. My baby and I can live very well for a good while off of this."

As she walked out of the restaurant, she was smiling and singing. "Reunited and it feels so good, reunited cause they understood, there's one perfect fit and sugar this one is it, they both are so excited cause they're reunited….

BORN NOT TO KNOW

"I don't know if I can do this, Michael," replied Jazz. "What if I get hurt or something?"

Michael shook his head in discontent. "You worry too much, Jazz. Do you think I would send you on a date that has not been fully vetted? A family man, who uses our services at least twice a month. And this fool is paid. Rhonda went out with him back in July and brought back two thousand in one night. So I say 'YES' he is a front-runner in the game."

Jazz let out a deep sigh. "Do I have to stay all night; I mean, this is my first date and all."

Michael sat down next to Jazz on the bed and gave her a sinister stare. "Stop making this hard for yourself, girl. Do you know how many young ladies would kill for an opportunity like this? You said that you needed the extra money so you can show your parents that you're independent, so they can trust you to do more things. What is this, your junior year in college? If you shut up and do like I tell you to do—after I get my cut—you can have the rest of your tuition paid in full by the end of this year. Quit acting like a damn baby and go get that money. Bernard will be bringing your car in forty-five minutes."

Michael went into his jacket pocket, pulled out a couple of Valiums and handed them to Jazz.

"Take these with a few crackers, this should mellow you out a bit. And like we discussed earlier, wear that beige London Fog trench coat and the matching stilettos, nothing else. The man says he will take care of the rest when you get there. I'll call to check on you in an hour or so, Jazz. Please don't make this ugly for the both of us."

Michael left, leaving Jazz to prepare for the evening. She did exactly as she was instructed, wearing only a coat and heels, with no clothing or undergarments beneath. She brushed her hair to the back, pulling it neatly into a ponytail; she donned hoop earrings and a thin coat of makeup and lipstick. *What kind of dude is this?* she thought to herself. *Requesting a younger woman in her early twenties with the ambiance of a teenager. Sick bastard.*

Bernard texted Jazz to let her know he was in the parking lot. She took a Valium, accompanied by Saltines and grape juice; then, grabbing her purse from the nightstand, she sent up a small prayer before leaving the apartment.

The drive to Winston-Salem seemed slightly longer than the norm. "I wonder why Michael couldn't set the date up in Charlotte," she mumbled. "I need to be compensated for mileage."

As she proceeded on, she noticed the sign for Winston-Salem. *Twelve miles out,* she thought. "There's a BP station on the next exit. I can stop there and freshen up."

Heading back to her car, Jazz receives a call from Michael. "How far out are you?" he asked. "You didn't run into any problems, did you?" Jazz explained that she pulled off to use the washroom and was now back on the road. "That's good," replied Michael. "Dudes like this don't like to be kept waiting. We're trying to get as much bread as we can. Send me a text when you arrive at the Kimpton-Cardinal; I'll then let Mr. G know you've arrived. You still have the paper I gave you with the info on it, don't you?"

Jazz let Michael know that she was all set but getting nervous by the minute.

"I gotta go, Mike, just ready to get this night over with."

Traffic in downtown Winston was atrocious. *Where in the world are all of these people going? Jazz thought to herself. It's ten thirty on a Monday evening.* She finally made it to her destination.

"This trick has WONDERFUL TASTE," she laughed. I've heard about this place. The Kimpton is the cat's meow! Might not be so bad after all."

After tipping the valet, she took out the information that Michael had provided, so she could know exactly where she was going. Ninth floor, room 919; across from the discus aquarium inside the wall.

"This place has glass elevators," she whispered. "Amazing."

Jazz shook her head in disdain—there were so many well-to-do patrons at the hotel that night. People who were out living their "best lives" while she was there to simply fulfill a desperate old man's geriatric fantasy. THE IRONY....

Feeling her nerves and her conscience getting the best of her, when she reached the ninth floor, she took a seat on a marble bench outside of the elevator door. She texted Michael two simple words—*I've arrived.*

A few minutes later, he texted a reply. *He's waiting on you. I'll reach out to you in a couple of hours to see how things are going. It's going to be fine. I'm very proud of you. If you play your cards right, you'll go far in this organization; might even become a "bottom girl."*

Per instructions on the paper, she opened her coat so that she was fully exposed and took the ponytail out of her hair. Knocking three times, a male voice on the other side of the door replied, "Come on it, it's open."

"Oh my God, for the love of Christ!" screamed Jazz as she dropped her phone, keys, and purse to the floor. Stumbling over her own feet, she propped herself against a small table in the corner of the dimly lit room. She grabbed her face, disgusted and in disbelief.

"Daddy, what the hell are you doing here?"

THE 11ᵀᴴ COMMANDMENT

Forward: The setting is in the early 1900s—Somewhere near the Georgia/Florida line.

The dialect and tone are from a different era; written for the day, for the time. This is "Country Folklore" with a western theme; not to be taken in offense; simply fiction with a "twist."

ENJOY!

"I've been telling you all week to get rid of that horse, Joe. Just the thought of knowing he's in that barn makes me sick." Zora went on and on about her discontentment with her husband's horse. Joe, who didn't make a fuss, continued to ignore her as he read the daily press. "Woman, like I've been tellin' you for days, the horse is staying and that's final. You must be crazy to think that I am just gonna throw my horse away after winnin' it fair and square against Luther Morris at the Faro game, last Sunday. Not gonna happen." The two of them continued to go back and forth about the horse, when the phone rings. "Answer the phone, Zora," said Joe. "Old man Crater is supposed to be calling me for work later today and I can't miss it; an option to make a ton of cash before the cold weather sets in and I plan to do just that. Woman get the molasses out'cha ass and get the phone."

Zora put down her wash basket and did as she was told. When she picked up the receiver the phone was immediately disconnected. "I guess they must've had the wrong number Joe, as soon as I picked it up nobody was there."

"It figures," mumbled Joe. "The very time I'm lookin' for something, people start playing on the phone. Zora, you need to get over to Neeley's and get that washin' done. The very thought of you doing those folks' laundry makes me want to puke. That's why I am trying to get my hands on somethin' so you won't have to work like a dog no more."

Zora turned to face her husband with a searing rage.

"If you stayed on a job and quit gamblin' off everything we have, I wouldn't have to work at all. Losing my hard-earned bits and the most you got was an old devil horse, just behooves me. That horse ain't staying here, Joe, I mean it."

Joe emerged from the table and stood face-to-face with Zora. "Woman, I don't think I've made myself clear to you. You better not bother that horse. In time, I plan on makin' a lot of money off of that coney. I haven't shown you who the man of the house is in a long while; it's about time I…."

Zora looked at Joe with the eye of a dog. "If you so much as raise a finger to me Joe Henry, that will be the LAST thing you ever do in this lifetime. I'm puttin' the man on you; yeah, that's right. Get you some time up in the 'workhouse' where you can fight all day and night if you want to. Try it and see. I'm beggin' you."

Joe knew his wife was serious and he walked away. "I ain't got no time to be fightin' with you, woman, got money to make."

Zora grabbed her wash basket and proceeded to the Neeley's for work.

After an honest day of work, Zora made it home safely and retired to the porch to catch her breath. "I am so tired," she whispered to herself. "There has got to be a better way of life than this." Standing to her feet, she was stifled by the sounds of neighing and rustling coming from the barn. Letting her curiosity and nosiness get the best of her, Zora walked swiftly to the barn. Slowly pulling the door ajar, she noticed the piercing white horse in the back of the barn, standing against the wall. It stood gallantly, with its tail swaying back and forth. The horse caught sight of Zora, staring blankly with an angry scowl. The horse sensed the aggravation from the woman and dropped to its knees; as if it was humbling itself to take whatever lashing that was coming its way.

Zora frowned. "That's right. You better kneel in front of me. You won't be here past this evenin' old devil horse with red eyes. You are evil and you don't belong around here. I can't get Joe to see it, but having you here is a sign of somethin' terrible. I just know it." Zora slammed the barn door shut and thought about how she was gonna rid their property of the horse. "I'll just get Joe full of "Toddies" this evenin' after supper." she laughed. "I'll cut the horse loose then."

During supper, Joe was complaining to Zora about how Old Man Crater only gave him half of his pay and promised him the rest before Saturday. "Can you believe that old man?" screamed Joe. "I raked leaves, busted bricks, laid shingles, and chopped wood; didn't even have time to eat my lunch. I told him that my pay this week, better add up to two hundred bits or somebody's going to hell." Joe handed the hundred bits that he made to Zora; and she placed it in the mason jar that she used to save coins and bits for hard times. "Zora," he said sullenly. Help me off with my boots, if you will." Zora handed her husband a flask of whiskey toddy and she watched in awe as he guzzled it down; as if it were his last drink this side of mankind. After removing his boots, Joe asked for another toddy; and another one. Zora did as she was told without hesitation. Minutes later, she had Joe just where she wanted him; passed out and leaned back in his chair, SNORING.

"I can make my move now," she mumbled. "That horse is out of here."

Zora slipped on her water boots, grabbed the wicker broom and lantern for light. She was careful not to arouse Joe; this wasn't the time to fight with him. Making it to the barn, she noticed how still the wind had become and the quiet was deafening. This time she showed no false modesty. She flung open the barn door and there stood the horse, whinnying as if it knew the worst was yet to come. The horse was tied to a rafter by a rope. Finding a small step stool in the corner, Zora propped herself up to untie the loops. Noticing that it was free, the horse shook his head and lunged forward. Zora gave the coney three swats on its rearend with the broom. Fervently, the horse stood upright on its hind-legs, bucking and raring.

"Get!" yelled Zora. "Leave this place, demon." She gave the horse a few more swats; and like a bolt of lightning, it made its way to the door, striking out into the darkness, taking no prisoners.

Inside the house, Joe was slowly coming around, but drunkenly stumbled to his feet upon hearing the screams from the horse that was running back and forth throughout the yard. Grabbing his shotgun, Joe made a mad dash to the side of the house; this is where he sees Zora flinging rocks towards the now livid animal.

"I told you to get!" she screamed. "Get off my land!" Joe, who was taken aback by his wife's actions, pushes Zora to the ground as she tries to grab the shotgun. "Shoot him, Joe, shoot him. Don't you see this horse means us no good?" Joe drops the gun and begins to try and wrestle the horse to the ground; to no avail, the horse breaks loose and makes off into the woods. Joe grabs his head in anguish as he looks at Zora in disbelief. "I will deal with you another time woman, you really done it this time, Zora."

Zora scurries to her feet as she tried to grab Joe's arm. "It's for the best, Joe," she cried. "Let him be. Let him go. We will get another horse before winter. You know Mr. Jonesby in Jacksonville let's his go 'two for one' sometimes. We will be alright, Joe; please let it be." Zora's pleas meant nothing to Joe as he scampered into the house, grabbing his knapsack and a handful of shells for his shotgun.

"Don't do this, Joe; leave that horse alone!" screamed Zora. "It if means that much to you, we can take what we have now, go into town tomorrow, and get another one."

Joe pushed Zora to the wayside. "I'm going after my horse," he snarled. "He's a smart horse. I know he went right back to where I got him from. I'll be back before dusk tomorrow; and don't forget you got it comin' when I get back. Not even the 'man' is gonna be able to save you from what I got for you. If you know what's best, you won't be here."

As the night passed swiftly, Zora laid on her front porch, longing for just a mere glimpse of Joe—who was now gone for more than twelve hours. As the sun rose and set, Zora made a few phone calls to neighboring townsfolk, alerting them to what happened and Joe's absence. They offered their assistance by coming to sit with Zora, praying and chanting. About a quarter past the ninth hour, one of the townsmen noticed a funnel of dust moving quickly from the pasture. He beckoned for Zora and the rest of the neighbors to flock to the yard, as they yearned to see what was coming towards them. "It's Joe!" screamed Zora. "He's back, he's back."

As the presence grew closer, one of the neighbors shouted, "It looks like a horse, a brown horse, and it's heading this way."

Everyone spread out as they awaited the horse to clear the yard. "Grab him, grab him! cried Zora. Something is strapped to his back and on its tail." The men were able to get the horse stopped, then they noticed what was strapped to the horse's back was a baby.

"Wait a minute, screamed one of the neighbors, get that knapsack off the horse's tail; Stand back, people, stand back."

One of the townswomen grabbed the baby, and Zora grabbed the knapsack. She quickly opened the sack and made a GRUESOME discovery. It was Joe's severed head with a note attached.

Zora fell to her knees and wept aloud. One of the townspeople grabbed the note.

It read:

"Zora, I hated to do this to you, but I had no other choice. That rotten husband of yours had it comin' to him for a very long time. For months, I sat back and said nothin' as he frolicked around town with my wife; knocked her up too. And yes, that is Joe's baby boy. Had the nerve to show back up here to take my white horse; the one he STOLE from me last Sunday. Couldn't have been nothin' but fate. But I give him credit, he was a bold one.

"Zora, you are a good woman, always have been. The least I could do was send your husband's 'bastard child' and another horse over there; oh, and his HEAD so you can give him a proper burial. Trust me, I did my wife the same way; butchered her and sent her HEAD to her mother up in Eatonville, it should get there any day now."

The 11th Commandment—Thou shall not covet thy neighbor's "wife nor horse" or you will be reduced to a HEAD….

ARCTIC MEMORY

Glenda checked the time on her cell phone. *I'm going to be late,* she thought to herself. *Of all days, my car decided to conk out—so I'm stuck riding public transportation at 5:50 A.M.; it's twenty-two degrees out here.*

Glenda felt the sting of the wind against her lips. She remembered that she had just purchased a tube of Chapstick the day before. As she searched her pocketbook for the lip balm, she was startled by a young man standing under the light pole across the street.

"How are you today?" he asked. "Cold out here, isn't it?"

Glenda nodded in agreeance.

"Haven't seen you around before," replied the man. "Do you catch the bus here often?"

The frigid temperatures made it impossible for Glenda to carry on a conversation with the man, so she shook her head "no" to answer his question.

"There are usually at least, ten to twelve people out here by now." He laughed. "I guess the hawk was a bit much for them today. I love the cold weather; you get used to it after a while."

The young man went on for minutes, rambling about the weather and shouting at cars and trucks passing by. " Slow down woman, wherever you're trying to go, it will be there when you make it; hey dude, get off the freakin' cell phone, that's how innocent people get killed. Pay attention."

"This man has some serious issues," Glenda mumbled. "I pray the bus comes soon or I might have to call in to work."

Glenda checked her cell phone again.

There is no way I'm gonna make it to Westridge before seven, she thought. *I might as well call it a day.*

Just as she was about to phone her job, she noticed the young man sprawled out on the ground in front of the light pole.

"Not today," she whispered. This can't be happening."

When the young man appeared to not be breathing, Glenda called out to him.

"Hey, guy… hey; are you alright?" the young man did not respond.

Glenda used a few choice words and proceeded across the street to check on him.

"Are you okay?" she wailed "I'm calling an ambulance."

With the wind picking up rapidly, Glenda accidentally drops her cell phone. There was black ice on the ground, causing the phone to slide downwards, by the end of the block.

"This is all I freakin' need," she said. "This birdbrain is passed out on the cold ass concrete, the bus is almost thirty minutes late, I pray that my phone is still working, and I may have to miss work. I don't want to ask, what else?"

Glenda finally was able to get to her phone, when she noticed the bus coming towards her stop. Slipping and sliding, she was trying to flag the bus down; but of course, it kept right on going.

"Grabbing her head, she looked back in an attempt to check on the young man.

She noticed there was only a tennis shoe lying against the pole.

"What the fuck!" she screeched. "All of this unnecessary bullshit and the dude gets up and leaves his shoe. I missed my damn bus trying to help him… I just—"

"My brother missed his bus trying to help somebody too," a male voice replied.

Glenda turned in the direction of the voice and stopped dead in her tracks.

She was standing right across from the exact replica of the young man; only difference was, this guy was wearing a suit.

"Please don't be alarmed," he said. "We were twins. This is actually the ninth anniversary of his passing; he was killed by a teen driver texting on his cell phone; my brother was trying to give a homeless man directions to the night shelter, when the careless driver jumped the curb and smashed him into that light pole. Hit him so hard, the impact knocked off one of his shoes. Trust me, you're not the only one who has seen him. I place the shoe by the pole every December since his death, to honor his memory since that's all my family has left. He really acts up this time of the year."

Always remember, those who die bad—don't stay in the ground.

I PROMISE I'LL BE A GOOD BOY

"I really appreciate you ladies giving me a ride," said Tony. I've been walkin' for several hours; I was about to catch a charley horse. It's a long way back to Eatonville."

Gina and Valerie continued to converse with the young man as they continued down Highway Four into Orange County.

"This is something we normally don't do," replied Valerie. "Picking up hitchhikers can be very dangerous, but by you being so young and well mannered, we couldn't just leave you out there all alone. Besides, we're going through Eatonville anyway; we live in Kissimmee."

Tony smiled. "So what were you ladies doing up this way. You have family here?"

"Just chillin' at Daytona Beach for the weekend," laughed Gina. "Question is, what are you doing up this way? What are you about thirteen, fourteen years old? Your family let you travel out here by yourself?"

"It's a very long story," he sighed. "That's why I am truly trying to get home. I appreciate you ladies so much. This is a very nice car; it must belong to one of your boyfriends."

"Listen to you," cried Valerie. "Already coming into your chauvinistic ways. You don't think a lady can own a car like this? But since you must know, it belongs to my brother."

"I figured that," replied Tony. "This car has way too much horsepower for the average female. It's one of my favorites."

"We have several sandwiches and snacks in the cooler if you're hungry," said Gina. "Take as many as you'd like. They're just gonna go to waste anyway. We should be makin' it to Eatonville in about twenty minutes."

The young man took the ladies up on their offer and helped himself to a couple of turkey sandwiches and a bottle of apple juice. "This is the best treatment I've received in a long time," said Tony. "I miss my mother's cookin'. I can't wait to get home."

•   •   •

"He sure was a nice young man, replied Gina. I wonder what he was doing by himself, so far away from home and no way to get back...."

The ladies drove the rest of the way in silence, heading back to Kissimmee.

"Hey, Val," said Gina. "Tony left his jacket in the backseat last night. They predicted heavy rain and high winds in Orlando and Eatonville in the next few days. I think we should get his jacket back to him before nightfall."

The two ladies agreed.

"It was so dark out here last night, Val," said Gina. "Are you sure this is the house?"

"I'm positive," replied Gina. "I remember the white van in the driveway."

Valerie grabbed the jacket and proceeded to the front door.

A lady answered. "How may I help you?" she asked.

"Good afternoon, ma'am. My name is Valerie and that's my friend Gina in the car. Last night around nine thirty or so, we dropped a young man off here named Tony. He left his jacket in the backseat of our car and we wanted to return it to him."

The woman stood puzzled. "Who did you say you dropped off here last night?" she asked. "You must be mistaken."

Valerie was at a loss for words. "Ma'am, I know this is where we dropped him off. I remember the van in the driveway. Is he home? I just wanted to return the jacket to him—"

"Young lady!" cried the woman. "If this is some kind of joke, then it isn't the least bit amusing. And where on earth did you get that jacket?"

The woman snatched the jacket from Valerie's hand and slammed the door.

As she was walking back to the car, she noticed a young girl standing at the end of the driveway beside the mailbox.

"Tony was my brother," whispered the girl. "He died three years ago. That was the jacket he was wearing when he left the house heading to Daytona Beach with some friends. He wasn't supposed to go because he couldn't swim and there was no parental supervision. He went anyway; he disobeyed my mother. He wouldn't listen.. He just wouldn't listen…. You really shouldn't have come here and upset us like this."

Valerie shook her head. "My friend and I dropped Tony off at this house last night. If this is your way of letting us know that he no longer lives here, then we get it. We'll leave. No need to go to the extreme."

From inside the house, the woman overheard the conversation between her daughter and Valerie. She is hesitant, but makes her way outside.

"Wait a minute," said the woman. "It's obvious that you can't take no for an answer. The both of you are welcome to come with us if you'd like."

The woman grabbed her daughter's hand.

Valerie looked inside the car at Gina. Shrugging her shoulders, she locked the car and they both followed quickly on foot behind the woman and little girl.

"Since you wouldn't leave well enough alone," cried the woman. "Welcome to our reality." She nodded towards a grave in the middle of the cemetery.

The two young women grabbed their heads in disbelief. Valerie fell to her knees in dismay. "This can't be happening!" cried Gina. "He was just in our car."

On the weather-beaten headstone it read:

Bryson Antonio Westbrook (Tony)

Our dearly departed…

Deuteronomy 27:16 "Cursed is he who dishonors his father and mother. "

And at the very bottom of the stone, there was a half-eaten turkey sand-wich; along with an empty bottle of apple juice….

PROVERBS 31 WOMAN

"It was very thoughtful of Pastor Nicks to lead the service for us today on such short notice," said Sister Mathis. "Our prayers are with you First Lady, being that Reverend Banks is down in his back right now."

The two ladies conversed for a short while as Pastor Nicks was bringing his sermon to a close.

"As we go about our way this afternoon, let us pray for the shepherd of this congregation; Reverend Pernell Banks, as he is battling with pain in his extremities. Let him regain his strength and valor to fight against the arthritis demon that is trying hard to infiltrate his body. Let the regimen of medications and rest, along with prayer be the cocktail that he needs to embrace a speedy recovery. We will also pray for the First Lady of this parsonage, Arlinda Banks as she holds down the fort, standing high where her husband has fallen low. Lord we ask that she is granted peace, strength, and serenity because we know that this task is not an easy one. This is also very hard at this time because the First Lady is "with child." But, Heavenly Father, You said in Hebrews 13:5— You will not leave us nor forsake us; and I know that You will see this family through—and we will hold You to Your promise.…

"For His namesake that we pray which is Christ Jesus—we thank God and Amen."

After the final offering, the parishioners thanked Pastor Nicks for his service as everyone departed the sanctuary. Looking back, Sister Mathis noticed the First Lady sitting on a pew holding her stomach.

"Are you feeling okay, First Lady?" she asked. "Can I get you some water or something?"

The First Lady shook her head no.

"I'm fine, Sister Mathis," she replied. "I'm getting closer to my sixth month and this little joker is starting to kick more and more. My mother said since I'm carrying the baby up high, it's a boy. The Reverend and I sure hope it is."

Sister Mathis smiled. "Well, with that being said, let me get one of the deacons to help you to your car. A few of the sisters (including myself) got together and cooked you all some food for a few days; that should take some of the pressure off of you and the Reverend; not having to worry with cookin'."

The First Lady obliged everyone for their good deeds and gave instructions on services for the following week.

"We must pray that the Reverend is at least somewhat better, so he can be here on Wednesday. He has a doctor's appointment tomorrow. Let's stay encouraged."

The First Lady grabbed her stomach again. "With the way this child is kickin', he is ready to move the Reverend right out of the pulpit. By Grace, see you all on Wednesday."

The First Lady thanked the neighborhood kids for helping her bring the food into the house; she gave them each a dollar.

"You guys try not to make so much racket outside; my husband is upstairs sleeping. He's not feeling well."

In the kitchen, she noticed that everything was just as she left it. Even the breakfast plate she had fixed for her husband was untouched, and the "Mahalia" was still blaring in the background.

I would have canceled service altogether if I'd known he was feelin' this bad, she thought to herself. *Let me get up there and check on my husband.*

In her delicate condition, walking up the stairs felt like an eternity. When she finally reached the top, she placed her Bible and cell phone on the small table just outside her bedroom door; and leaned against it for several seconds to catch her breath.

When she entered the bedroom, she heard the shower running in the bathroom.

"Good. He's finally up," she mumbled. "Now, we can go downstairs and eat because I'm so—"

She was startled by the sound of two voices.

"We gotta hurry up; you know Arlinda will be back soon. I don't know how I let you talk me into coming into your wife's...."

The First Lady backed up slowly towards the door, almost tripping over her own feet. She stumbled into the table in the hallway. Remembering the .38 that she kept for protection in the bottom compartment of the table, she grabbed the gun and moved quietly towards the bathroom. Opening the door abruptly, she closed her eyes and fired four shots into the silhouettes behind the closed shower curtain....

Grabbing her aching stomach, she looked down to notice she was standing in a puddle of her own blood; reaching for her cell phone, she placed a call to 911.

"Hello, can you please send an ambulance? My name is Arlinda Banks. I think I'm having a miscarriage."

As she placed the weapon inside the Bible on the 23rd Psalm....

THE CRAZIEST THING

Janella stood looking at herself in admiration as she prepared for her first day as lead instructor of the GED classes down at Langston Prep. It had been two years since she entered a classroom, given that her life took an unexpected turn. Placing everything that she worked for on hold.

She picked up her pocket Bible from the nightstand and turned to the Philippians 4:13.

She nodded in agreement, grabbed her briefcase and headed on her way.

Before class convened, Janella and a few of the other instructors were in the lounge discussing what lay ahead.

"I have fifteen on my roster," said Brian. "Mostly at-risk teens and welfare moms."

"Consider yourself lucky," laughed Kendra. "I have twelve on mine and they all are new parolees. Some of 'em just got out a month ago. What about you, Janella? What does your list look like?"

Janella popped in a MENTOS and shook her head.

"I know I have seven. Didn't have a chance to look over their history yet. Just trying to get these next four months over with so this can be done."

"I understand," said Brian. "It's been a minute since you've been behind these walls. I know you'll be fine. You were one of the best instructors we had. I'm sure nothing has changed."

Janella introduced herself before she called roll.

My name is Janella Bentoncourt. If there is anyone in here over the age of thirty please feel free to call me Janella: otherwise I am Ms. Bentoncourt to the rest of you. Class starts promptly at three; not a minute later or a minute before. There are four hours to this session, and the only way you are allowed to leave without incident, is if you have either a medical emergency or something involving loss of life. Otherwise, what's missed is missed and you can either deal with it or get notes from your neighbor. I will not repeat myself. I encourage full class participation; just as you report to me four days a week, I also have to report your progress or digress to my boss every week. All cell phones need to be silenced during sessions and are only allowed to be accessed for educational purposes while in class. If you need to take a call or answer a text during class, send me a SKYPE message and once acknowledged, feel free to exit the room. Snacks and drinks should be kept to a minimum and conversations of any kind, unless it is particularly addressing the subject matter of our assignment, should be limited in nature and not for the entire class to hear. Now that I have set the rules of the house, let's see who we have with us today."

"Michael Daniels…. Here

James Reed… Present

Ursula Mitchell… Present

Tori Vincent… Here

Logan Fikes… Here

Eric Nash… Yes

Avis Bentoncourt—"

Janella could not believe the last name she had just read. She repeated the name again and did not receive a response.

"I believe that was the chick that stepped out right before you came in," replied Michael. "I think she left to make a phone call. Her phone charger and bag are still on the desk, so she should be coming back."

Janella was at a loss for words and was paralyzed with racing thoughts.

The door opened. In walked a young woman, embarrassed because she had interrupted class and apologetically took her seat.

Janella forced herself to speak. "Avis," she said. "I know you thought you would never have to cross my path again. Were you outside talking to Pharodd? Next time you talk to him, let him know that the check he sent for his daughter (our daughter's) private school bounced this month and although I went ahead and paid it, he needs to run me my six hundred dollars."

Avis could not lift her head up due to shame. "Janella, this is really not a conversation that you and I should be having. You might need to take that up with Pharodd."

The entire class stood still. Janella, regained her composure and heeded Avis's advice. She thought back to Philippians 4:13, smiled and went ahead with class, not appearing at all phased by the snide remark of the young woman.

"Class was good today, people. Remember when we meet tomorrow, I need that assignment on naming all of the fifty states, including each capital and their most valuable resource. Do not come back to my class if it's not completed. No excuses."

One of the students, Logan, stayed behind to address Janella when everyone had left.

"Ms. Bentoncourt, I just wanted to commend you for how you handled that situation today in class. You came off like a real "G." I don't know what's going on and it's not my business—"

"You're right," replied Janella. "It's not your business and I would appreciate if you would keep our conversations strictly on education. I am sorry you all had to witness that. It won't happen again. I PROMISE YOU."

Minutes later. the sound of broken glass disrupted the atmosphere of calm. Students and faculty ran from their classrooms to the front of the building.…

"Janella, please. We can talk about it. I had no idea you were teaching classes up here at Langston. She wouldn't have never enrolled here if I'd known that. Come on Janella, give me the crowbar."

Janella, closed her eyes, bit her bottom lip and hit Pharodd in the head with all of her might.

He fell to the ground on all fours, blood oozing from the top of his right ear.

Brian, her coworker from earlier, grabbed Janella by the arm and wrestled the crowbar out of her hand. "It's over, J. it's over. Come on now. You proved your point."

Janella glanced over to Avis, who was standing beside the car overwhelmed by fear and grief.…

Janella smiled and looked down on Pharodd.

"Yeah, your wife told me to take it up with you, so I did. You thought I was gonna let that mess go, Pharodd? The public humiliation, the mental anguish, leaving me and your two kids almost BANKRUPT for a woman who doesn't even have a GED…..

She shook her head and laughed. "I can do ALL things through Christ who strengthens me."

POSSUMS

"We've been over this time and time again," said Gordon. "Miles, you're a very nice guy. You've been through a lot over the years, but look at everything you've accomplished. Completing your bachelors, landing that great job at Fryson's and purchasing a new home, all within seven years. That is something definitely worth smiling about."

The four friends continued to converse and play cards, discussing everything from politics to life's problems.

"That's easy for you to say," laughed Miles. "Look at you. You made partner with Smith and Hartsfield, you've bought three homes and are renting out two of them, been married to that fine-ass Vanessa for over a decade now, and have two wonderful kids. Hell, I can't keep a woman more than six months."

"And your Spades game is off too," yelled Barry. "That's the second time you've re-nigged tonight. You might need to lay off that Crown and Coke."

A few minutes later, Gordon's daughter, Joni, came into the den to address her father.

"Hi, Daddy." She smiled. "I drew this for you today in Arts and Crafts." She presented a picture of himself, sitting in his office with his feet on the desk, sipping coffee. "This is you at work." She laughed. "Hope you like it."

Gordon grabbed his daughter, hugging her tightly. "Daddy loves it," he replied. "I will take it to the office tomorrow in a frame and hang it directly in front of my desk; so I can always see it. Now give Daddy a kiss."

After the display of affection, Gordon advised Joni that he was in the middle of entertaining adults and he will tuck her into bed shortly.

"Go find your brother, sweetheart, he's awfully quiet up there. I'll be up to put you guys to bed in a few."

Doing as she was told, Joni made sure she gave every man in the room a kiss on the cheek, referring to them each as "Uncle."

Miles shook his head. "Man, you have it made. What I wouldn't do to have your life."

The card game continued for a few hours more, when Gordon noticed the time.

"Let me make sure my kids are in bed. Vanessa will be home soon; and that's all I need to hear is that I didn't have them in bed on time. And don't be lookin' at my hand while I'm gone. You know I don't trust you, Otis."

The card players took a "break five" while Gordon attended to his kids.

Miles turned to Barry. "Don't you think you might need to call Yvonne? We all know it's past your bedtime and she keeps you on a short leash."

Miles and Otis gave each other some dap.

Barry smirked. "That's one of the reasons why you don't have a woman now, Miles. Always trying to talk mess about someone else's relationship. My lady and I get along great and our arrangement suits us just fine. It's a shame a dude like you has so much success in some areas and the biggest failure in the areas where it counts. Once the job, the fame, the cars, and the house is gone, what will you have left? It's terrible having all of those material possessions and no one to share it with. Quiet as it's kept, we only hang out with you because we feel sorry for you, bro—"

Miles sprang up from the table. "Feel sorry for me, dude! Is that what you said? Ya'll are only cool with me out of sorrow?" Miles grabbed his jacket and threw his set of cards onto the floor. "I don't need any of you. Feel sorry for me, man? I feel sorry for all of ya'll. While you're up here talkin' shit to me, Barry; everyone knows that Yvonne's been screwin' her boss for more than a year now, but keepin' tabs on your every move."

Otis gets to his feet. "Miles, man you are way out of line. That is wrong for you to say that about this man's wife. I'm outta here."

Miles blocks Otis's path. "Let's not up and leave now, we're just getting' started. Remember, you guys feel sorry for me, right? Otis, we all know that you've been stickin' really close up under Gordon these days. Yeah, you need him to help you pay your mortgage for the next few months; seems Carletta almost got your ass in the poor house with all of that damn gamblin'—"

Instantly, Otis hauls off and knocks Miles to the ground. "You're gonna keep my wife's name out of your mouth!" The three of them get into an all-out brawl… but their FURY came to a screeching halt, when they hear a paralyzing scream—emanating from upstairs.

Gordon stumbles wearily from the second floor, mortified and helpless. Tears streaming profusely down his cheeks.

In his arms, were the bodies of his lifeless eight-year-old son, Paxton, and four-year-old daughter, Joni clutching an empty bottle of **Lunesta**. Weak in the knees from grief, Gordon falls down the last few steps; a note that was in his shirt pocket written in third grade handwriting fell to the floor….

It read:

> **"We wanted to surprise Mommy by being asleep when she got home, so we can go to FUN-TOWN on Saturday with Aunt Denise.**
>
> **Love You,**
> **Pax and Joni**

Callously, Gordon looked in the direction of Miles, who was standing in utter disbelief and shock. He quietly whispered, "Now, do you still want my life?"

DEAD WRONG

"You can't just keep us locked in here like this!" screamed Jasmine. When is this pandemonium going to end?" The students huddled together in a corner, wailing their concerns.

"This is hard for everybody, Jasmine," replied Mrs. Phipps. "There is an epidemic spreading in this city and the only way we can guarantee your safety is to keep you locked in this school."

There was a quick silence; the vice principal began to speak over the public address system. "Teachers, students, and other faculty. We just received an update on the current status of the outbreak plaguing our city at this time. Thirty-seven people confirmed dead, more than a hundred in grave condition. It is still a question as to how the virus is transmitted. The National Center for Disease Control has announced that it could possibly be airborne. Students, we have notified all of your parents and guardians and will keep you informed of the status of this dreadful crisis on an hourly basis."

"Just what we need," replied Chris. "Half of these people don't believe in taking baths. And to imagine being locked in here for God knows how long."

Everyone began to speak at once. This was going to be a very long day.

"Well, since we're all here," cried Mrs. Phipps, "this would be a great time to go over the information for this semester's term paper. The subject for this year's thesis will be about what body part do you think you can live without."

The students burst into laughter. "You're joking, right?" asked Jasmine. "This city is about to declare a state of emergency and you want us to ponder over what limb we can stand to lose?"

In that instant, the notification for the public address system was blaring.

"Attention all teachers, students, and faculty. We now have another update on the outbreak situation. There have been six more confirmed deaths, raising the total to forty-three. People I urge you to stay away from the windows and do not go anywhere near the doors. Try to save as much battery life with your cell phones and tablets; to reach out to your family regarding evacuation procedures, once we are notified. The governor is about to announce a statewide emergency, so teachers please enable your projector screens for viewing. The broadcast will take place in roughly ten minutes, so let's prepare ourselves. I will come back on momentarily to discuss lunch procedures."

Everyone began to whisper to themselves, hoping and praying that their loved ones were not among the casualties.

"I know that the VP has notified all of our parents," said Jasmine. "But can we at least send a text to let them know that we're alright and safe thus far? Mrs. Phipps, you need to reach out to your husband as well. We don't know how long we'll be confined. We just need to let them know that we're safe and vice versa."

Mrs. Phipps nodded.

"After the governor's address, I'll allow you all to send one text; we have to make sure that everybody's phone has enough power, if we have to be here longer than today. I hope that everyone has their chargers."

After the governor's address, you could hear the screams of several students throughout the school.

"Now they're saying that we could be locked down for seven days or longer!" screamed the crowd. "What are we supposed to do for clothes, hygiene supplies? Some of us have medical situations that require certain treatments and medications."

The students went on and on with their hysteria. Mrs. Phipps knew the students had a valid point, but she was stuck there like everybody else. She also had a husband and a three-year-old son that she was insanely worried about. But what more could she do?

The vice principal finally made the announcement about the procedures for lunch.

"Lunch will be administered according to grade level with no more than thirty-five minutes allowed per grade. For any of you who decide to get a "wild hair" and try to leave, ALL doors have been double padlocked from the inside. This is serious, young people; **it has been stated that this plague is airborne and we cannot take the risk of something deadly happening to you on our watch**. This affects all of us."

In the cafeteria, the workers were complaining because they were also away from their children and families in the wake of this terrible epidemic.

"They want us to be here to make sure their kids are fed, while we know nothing that is going on with our own," said Alberta. "It's just not fair."

"Don't worry about it, Alberta," laughed Paul. "Remember, we are the lowly food service workers—underpaid and disrespected all the time. Trust me, it will be all over soon."

As he continued to stir the cyanide into the green beans, he said, "Yes, it will be all over soon—**airborne** my ass.…"

9 7 9 8 8 8 8 1 2 2 3 6 5